Tim Cooks

Tim Cooks is a gestalt entity - for this book he was comprised of the following students from Wilmington Academy:

- ◇ Bethany Bennett, age 13
- ◇ Courtney Richards, age 11
- ◇ Haig Spalding, age 12
- ◇ Hidayah Mustafa, age 14
- ◇ Katie Sharp, age 11
- ◇ Katy Smith, age 14
- ◇ Laura Ash, age 11
- ◇ Ryan Jones, age 14
- ◇ Ryan King, age 13
- ◇ Sam Homewood, age 11
- ◇ Tommy Talyor, age 13

who were overseen by Krista Veysey and Joseph Reddington.

The group cheerfully acknowledge the wonderful help given by staff at:

⋄ Wilmington Academy

⋄ Royal Holloway College

⋄ UnLld

The cover was provided by Donata Besa and Stephen Eate, who are also students at Wilmington Academy, and they were overseen by Frank Fiorentino.

The group started deciding the plot of the novel at 0900 on Monday 5th December 2011 and completed their last proofreading by 1020 on Friday 9th December 2011. Within the body of the text we can honestly say that every word of the story, every idea, every character and, yes, every mistake is entirely their own work. No teachers, parents or other students touched a single key during the process, and we would ask readers to read it with this in mind. The only parts that have been edited are this preface and the author biography sections at the back of the book.

We at the school stand amazed at what a group of secondary school students can put together in four-and-a-bit days, and we hope you will too.

Deception of Success

Tim Cooks

December 13, 2011

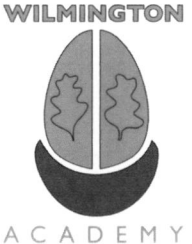

Contents

1 Start 9

2 Darren's Enlightenment 17

3 Successful Revelation 23

4 The Dilemma Starts 33

5 A Request 39

6 The Test 45

7 The Pleading Beg 49

8 Approached 55

9 The Struggle 61

10 An Inspiring Resolution	67
11 Agreement	73
12 Let the Bullying Commence	81
13 Nice Day at the Market	89
14 Silent Treatment	99
15 The Inadequate is Informed	103
16 The Bullying Continues	107
17 Time for Answers	111
18 Confrontation	115
19 Family Affairs	119
20 The Lost Loved One	123
21 Getaway	131

22 The Saviour	**135**
23 . . . and. . .	**141**
24 Disaster Strikes	**143**

Chapter 1

Start

Location: Coborn Street by Victoria Park in London.
Time: 7/6/2011 Monday 10:00pm.

"Quick, Dan! Pass me the rest of the boxes before the police come and get us! We need to get the rest now and run!" A determined convict darted towards the back of a condemned van that consisted of adequate products, with the intention of thieving them. Four missionary teenagers unloaded the back of a packed van with goods that were about to be present in the same place no longer.

An elderly driver stumbled his way out of the van in order to knock on the door of a persistent character awaiting his shopping that would make his new house entirely complete.

It was a conventional day in the city of London and criminals were striking once again; there were police patrolling the streets like a spokesman lost for words.

As one would have expected, four teenagers were attempting a fatal crime that could leave all of them in prison.

When it had finally come to realization that boxes were being unloaded from the back of his van, the driver turned around with incompetence as to only just noticing the items slowly, but gradually, going missing chronologically, in order of expense.

"Wait, you just stop right there! Remove one more item from my van and I will have all of you prosecuted!" With slight reluctance, the van driver darted towards the scene in which the teenagers were now attempting escape.

The victim driver had committed no wrong and yet he was being blamed for such incompetence of a high extent; the eager customer looked at the driver in disgust as she knew that she would not be receiving her items any time soon. Instead of helping the van driver, she decided upon yelling in disgrace, opposing the actions of the driver who was supposed to have been unloading all of the items off of the van into the house of the rich who was full of resolute as to having a full, polished house by the end of the day.

Seconds later, the van driver had still not seized his items as the teenagers all ran coordinately in order to make escape. It had not yet came to the realization of the policemen that there was a serious crime occurring as they spoke. There were approximately ten policeman patrolling one particular street at the time of the event. Yet none of them appeared to have been devoting their undivided attention to the crime that was causing a major outbreak.

"Come on Jordan, just keep on running! We have got enough, we need to get out of here!" One of the near future convicts bellowed at his companion in order to dictate instructions that were to be followed. The four of the trouble makers continued running and had absolutely no intention of getting caught.

"Police, police, quick, quick! Get them, all of them, they have stolen the entire contents of my van! You need to help me!" The helpless victim cried from head to toe while he was watching his life slip through his fingers the amount of disappointment he had at the sight of his repugnance was proving the better of him. He barely lifted his arm up with the amount of glum he had, and extended his finger to the direction of the youths.

"Get back here! You're under arrest, there's no way of escape now so just give yourselves up!"

With all resolute and enlightenment from other officers, this particular policeman was full of enthusiasm as to capturing the youths in order to discipline them once and for all, restraining the younger generation.

Omitting to all instruction, the teenagers continued to run away in order to succeed their plan, must be reorganized due to the extreme success they were already promoting.

The entire city must have heard the screams of horror from the van driver who was disabled as to running after the rapid youths who ran at the speed of light.

"You're paying for those missing items, every last one of them! If it had not have been for you being a useless lump of nothing. I would have had a complete house for my children to come home to tonight!"

The entire city was awoken from the catastrophe that was occurring on their doorsteps. Disgusted at the blame the van driver was being conducted, the crowd filled themselves with sympathy towards him due to the unexpected trauma that had occurred, without pursuing his power.

"I do apologize on their behalf, but there was nothing I could have done! It was entirely out of my hands."

Without a word of inspiration, the arrogant mother shut the door with immense force that reached the scale of colossal. Everybody continued their daily schedule turning a blind eye to it all.

"We're nearly there, we're nearly there! We just need to reach the building, top floor and lock the doors and then we have clear!"

One of the convicts whispered influentially to the other in order to make sure that everybody was on track in terms of knowing what the precise plan was. Without having been given the opportunity to object to reluctance, the ring leader, referred to as Jordan, led the team into yet another street, where three police officers continued to chase the four suspects. Little did the youths know, the police officers were just as determined as themselves which did not leave them with very high hopes.

It appeared from the perspective of many that the youths and the police officers happened to be chasing around the same buildings simultaneously with neither of them succeeding. A lot of shouting was occurring as the police were fighting their battle against crime.

"Stop right now, lads! You're not going to win this!" the policeman barked at the top of his voice, in hope of obedience. The four teenagers diverted into another street where they were out of sight from the public. The chase had only just begun...

Chapter 2

Darren's Enlightenment

Location: Busy market street in East Ham, in a cafe
Time: 8/6/2011 Tuesday 10:00am

The cafe was a family run business, with about roughly twenty seats, so quite small. The walls were brown with white corrugated wall at the top, there were windows at the front, with four tables and eight seats overlooking the busy market street. Darren is sitting by the window on his own, with a cup of coffee and a sandwich in his hand. The cafe is half full with builders in high visibility jackets

There is smoke coming from the window at the back of the kitchen where the main cooker was. The staff were serving the customers, bacon sandwiches, full English breakfasts, teas, coffees were all flying out of the cookery window into the main cafe seating and dining area.

Whenever Darren went out, he always wore casual clothes that would not draw any form of attention. He never liked to leave without his dog as his dog was his long term companion that was a huge part of his life. He went to the cafe to have a cup of coffee which would refresh his brain as to thinking about what we would do with his life in terms of careers.

The typical day bypassed when Darren went into a trance that lasted for a decent ten minutes, expanding his ability to think for a long duration. Without anticipation of doing so, it came to Darren's attention that he did not have to find a job, he could simply start one up with the help of his friends as they could be very perceptive when they collected themselves together. Darren quickly finished his coffee and sandwich, then waited outside for all of his friends to arrive. They took a while, but they eventually showed up at the cafe.

Darren thought that his friends and himself could work well together on a small market stall around London. Darren was just a typical young man, as common as it could have got. He never thought, during his younger years, that he could have the intention of starting up a business with his friends in order to make money for a living. With a beam of joy and a gasp of enlightenment, Darren decided that it was no use stirring about the idea independently, he would confer with his peers in order to make the idea a reality!

It had been a disturbing and haunting thought to begin with as Darren had never been considered an intellectual. He would always have pride in every day life, but never would he be the one to come up with such an idea that could turn his life around for good, as well as his friends' lives. This day was a saviour to Darren as he could finally exult in his own existence by appreciating the inner talent that everybody is said to be in possession of.

"What if they think that I am not at all being serious?"

The negative thoughts had to come tumbling in sooner or later as Darren was never established as a confident person. Regardless of all, Darren decided upon meeting his friends, come rain or shine. They meant more than just three peers who were there to make him laugh. From Darren's perspective, they were the people who could make their lives as well as Darren's life worthwhile.

"That's it, I will spend the remainder of today polishing my idea and tomorrow my idea will be out in the open!"

Darren completed his plan so it sounded promising, instead of sounding like an idea that a five year old girl thought of over night and wanted to act it out.

Chapter 3

Successful Revelation

Location: Outside the cafe, on the market street.
Time: 8/6/2011 Tuesday 5:30am

The cafe is located on the market street. The street where all the vendors are selling in the market has roughly ten stalls with two empty ones. The street is flooding with people, some just walking past on their daily commute to work, while others are stopping at the stalls, while others are stopping in the cafe for a coffee and meeting with their friends in the cafe. The vendors are selling everything from fruit and veg to dog food and cat food.

After having been through months of unemployment and without a career or day of brightness to look forward to, Darren found himself staring at the same four walls he had been for days. He was tired of living the same day-to-day regime, wasting his life away. Somehow, time seemed to run ten times slower. Having to wait ten times longer was a tedious chore.

Whilst listening to the birds suffocating the silence in a pleasant cafe, Darren contemplated and considered the idea of starting up his business that he had thought of earlier on in the cafe. Admittedly, he opposed the idea of starting up a business as a sole trader due to the fact that he believed that he would not have the time or the money to start up a business individually. In addition to his initial thinking, Darren decided upon letting the other members of the group be informed of the idea that Darren believed could have been approved of with ease.

After five minutes of polishing the idea of starting up a business, Darren confirms his plan as compulsory, wherever it could possibly fit into his daily schedule. Immediately, without any reluctance or second thoughts at all, Darren contacted his close friend Lou-Lou who was demanded to pass the news on to the two remaining group members. As she was entirely loyal to Darren and would do so much as break a leg for him, she contacted the other half of the group in order to arrange a vital meeting that would depend on a future career between the four of them.

It was eleven o'clock at night and Darren was watching paint dry. He made a sudden movement to himself that allowed him to refresh his mind to ensure that he was in reality, instead of dreaming of reality. After ten successful minutes in the bathroom having a wash, Darren mentally scanned the noise of his phone ringing, which told him that the call was urgent in order for someone to have the anticipation to call him so late at night. With a beam of enlightenment upon his face, Darren diverted to the living room where his phone was neatly placed on the table ready to be answered.

"Hello, is this Darren?" "Indeed it is, Lou-Lou! What's the verdict?" "I totally approve of your idea, it is legendary!" After five action-filled minutes had passed their farewells, the conversation came to a dramatic close as Darren flung himself onto the furniture with inspiration fulfilling his entire body.

As soon as twilight had arrived, Darren was already preparing himself for the laborious day ahead of him. Without having the will power to prevent himself from smiling, Darren allowed his feet to take him out of bed after just four hours of delightful sleep. Without any form of anticipation, Darren knocked his cup of tea all over the floor, which erased his smile completely due to the intense irritation that he was suffering from. After an hour of intense frustration, Darren exited the door where he found himself on the streets of London where he made a diversion to the direction in which the allocated cafe was where he would express his ideas fresh from the brain in order to broadcast them to his friends.

After the group of four were collected together in order to discuss their political plans as to how they are to run the business, they had a brief introduction from Darren as to why the business would be a good idea and roughly how they would go about it. It was eleven o'clock precisely and Darren welcomed his companions by inviting them to join and participate in the running of a business which Darren had thought of all by himself.

"I have had the most inspiring of ideas" declared Darren.

"We could make deals with other shops in order to sell the phones that are unable to be sold in shops as they are too expensive. We will then sell them at a cheaper rate, ensuring that we will still receive a reasonable profit for each of us. More ideas to the mixture would be great! Other than that, I don't see what is delaying us!"

Speech had failed the remaining three members of the group as they were amazed at the thought of jubilant feelings finally being able to be present in their lives, after all those years of worrying about having a career and making a living for themselves as well as future families that could have been possible from any minute.

The four of the ambiguous teenagers hunted for the missing piece to the puzzle as it did not quite seem possible to just start up a business right away- there always had to be a catch!

"We could not possibly have enough money to run our own stall and sell phones! We barely even have enough money to feed ourselves!"

The idea had not even been written on paper and yet Joe had already discovered something to criticise. They all pulled in together in order to make sure that they could solve every problem in order to accomplish their dream once and for all. It only took determination and work ethics in order to make sure that a dream could be made reality by a golden pathway.

"The business is a spectacular idea! Of course, there will be a huge struggle along the way, but I am sure that we can all pull through this difficult period of time in order to meet success of a high level, shining our colours!"

Darren made a finishing statement to reassure the group of the business' success due to the fact that he was the key character that had faith in the business right from the core of the heart.

"I still don't think that this is going to work. How will we even get the money to start up the business? This is all going to fall to pieces and I am not sure that I even want to be a part of the plan any more. Everything is going to go horribly wrong. Sorry, but I cannot have faith in this business when I know full well that it is not going to work out."

Joe did not have any intention or belief in the business for many reasons.

"We have to have faith in an oncoming plan first of all. It is called trial and improvement, Joe. Besides, what could we possibly lose if the business does not go to plan? We will just simply return to our conventional ways and I guess we will have to discover another unique way in which we will sell ourselves. No risk, no gain." For one second, Joe actually took into account what he was being told and gazed into the thin air with contemplation that could put an author to shame. It was mind-blowing how dedicated to thinking Joe could actually be when he put his mind to it.

After the idea of the business was discussed, Lou-Lou walked home with intention of discussing the idea to her friends even further. When it came to sudden attention that her phone had no battery remaining, she decided to dart back home to retrieve her phone charger.

Chapter 4

The Dilemma Starts

Location: Mike's room, in Newham house, (their house).
Time: 9/6/2011 Wednesday, 5:00am

Mike's room has jet black wallpaper with a ocean blue wardrobe, bed and chest of drawers. The windows are double glazed and twice the size of any normal ones.

After lou Lou returns home, she starts hunting for her charger There was a view of a massive, perfect grass green park with children playing on the swings and on the see-sore. There are clothes all over the floor such as underwear and clothes that he wore a week ago.

He has a double bed with blue bed sheet covers, and pitch black curtains. He has a big room, the biggest room in the house and his sister has very small room.

Lou-Lou searched her bedroom for 10 minutes and "where could it be?" "I have looked everywhere other than the hallway and Mike's room. I bet mike took it because I know I would never leave it in the hallway. I better check Mike's room. If he has taken it, he has a lot of answering to do. I've been looking for ages".

She searched Mike's room and couldn't find it anywhere. She thought to herself, "I have not checked under the bed yet or the wardrobe". So she searched the wardrobe.

She searched under his clothes in the bottom of the wardrobe and it's not there. She then checks the top of the wardrobe, but no luck at all. "I wonder if it is under the bed". She says rhetorically. So she checks under the bed, even though it is disgusting in there. "I hope I find it soon I really need it".

She searched under his bed and found all disgusting things under there. She screams because she put her hand in a mouldy old sandwich. By this point she was very stressed and feels extremely tired. she then thought to herself she should just give up but at that moment in time found a small black box. she shook the box and from it came a rattling noise then opened it, She wondered if she should open it or not. "I'll take the risk," she thought to herself.

An expression of excitement spread across her face. It is the charger. She was happy and she says "I Can't believe I finally found it!" And then took it out. With a confused face she said to herself "what is this?: Oh my gosh it's drugs!!!" she was not happy with mike one bit and was very angry and told herself "why would he do that. he must have been influenced by his mates or influenced by peer pressured into it" she just couldn't bring herself to believe that the drugs were his or he would be taking them.

She was furious with Mike. She tried to call him five times and then asked, "why won't he answer his phone? I am going to get so angry in a minute!" Lou Lou didn't know what to do. she was extremely worried about her brother even though they don't get along at the best of times.

Lou-Lou was overly stressed and thought to herself "I will find Mike! and when I do, he'll have so much to answer for!" she tried everything she could think of to get hold of her twin brother. Lou Lou was sick to her stomach with anger and disappointment.

Lou-Lou looked high and low for her brother she went to his friends houses but still no luck. Lou Lou even went as far to go to the market on west ferry road next to the isle of dogs. She couldn'tfind Mike anywhere and she was even more angrier than she was before. she suggested to herself "I wonder if he is at the park?" so she went to the park. Mike was nowhere to be seen at the park. Then he remembered he was going to his mates house for the day to play on the X box. So she went back home and waited for him to get home, and she went on the computer to play games.

Chapter 5

A Request

Location: Newham House in the kitchen.
Time: 11/6/2011 Friday 13:00pm.

The walls are white and blue tiled with nine purple cupboards with different ornaments in. Some is cutlery, while others is kitchen ornaments such as pots and pans. There is a very large orange fridge and freezer full to the brim with food. The oven is twice the size of any normal one. Everything is over sized, the food prep areas is more than large enough.

It had been a disturbing day in which

everybody was found preceding a strenuous occasion, that left them appreciating a second of silence, more than a block of gold. The rain was hitting the floor with so much force, making the floor almost shatter into pieces. It was like a pane of glass. Lou-Lou was feeling even more down than ever and she did not at all believe that she could run a business between the group of four without committing an illegal act.

Lou-Lou's friends and herself had briefly discussed running a business between them. Due to the fact that they were all suffering from immense difficulty, in retrieving the job as a society always supported stereotypical phrases. T

Lou-Lou finally felt the inner instincts in order to politely ask her father for money in a subtle manner that would hopefully persuade him into obliging.

"Father?"

"Yes, Lou-Lou? it better be some thing important because"

Her father looked worn at Lou-Lou as though she was five years old again, belittling Lou-Lou to an extent.

"The others and I are intending on running a business together. In order to give ourselves a title as employed teenagers. However, we do not have enough money in order to make the idea sufficient in reality. I don't suppose that you could lend me some money in order to make our dream possible?"

Charlie, Lou-Lou's concerned father, vaguely objected to the proposal, under the impression that his daughter was not merely telling the absolute truth, which challenged his trust in his own flesh and blood.

"So long as you are only spending the money on the business and are putting all of your commitment into the business, and that tour are not not going to splash it out on things for you. You are entitled to have the money for as long as you shall require. I am sure you will make something out of your life by using the money wisely. however, sometimes I do doubt whether or not I am making the right decision as to accepting such question."

Charlie gazed into his daughter's eyes, making five minutes of consistent eye contact that would create an awkward atmosphere that would leaving the pair of relations lost for words.

After the undefined staring contest, Charlie reached out for his wallet that was full of notes that were screwed up, having been in his pocket for a long duration. Charlie allowed his daughter to reach out for the notes and take them into her pocket in order to do what she had claimed she was doing with the money. With a smile stretching from ear to ear, Lou-Lou allowed her feet to take her out of the portal that led to her own bedroom where she could keep the money safe in a locker where she would later meet with her friends in order to establish the good news.

Lou-Lou had witnessed the late time on the clock with read nine 0'clock precisely, meaning Lou-Lou was almost late for a brief meeting with her long term companions, all eager to receive the positive news about how much money Lou-Lou had managed to rake up from her father. Unaware that illegal magnetic fields had taken their cause, the group were all jubilant towards the success of receiving enough money to get the business on its feet.

Chapter 6

The Test

Location: News agents in East Ham. Time: 12/10/2011 Saturday 12:30 pm.

The size of the shop is not to wide, it is longer than it is wide, with the counter at the front. At the front of the shop is the sign, it has white text, on a green background. the shop sells everything from sweets, to coca cola and beer. There is two isles full of merchandise.

Joe was on his way to the newsagents. He was wearing very rough clothes and he looked very tough, menacing and conspicuous. When he met up with Layton who looked quite smart. He was wearing a sophisticated jacket and trousers that were quite posh, and Joe decided upon testing Layton to see if he was telling the truth about his ability to read. Joe knew that Layton couldn't read, but he just didn't want to tell the truth due to his low self esteem and introverted personality.

Joe is still not certain about Layton's ability to read and therefore sends him into the newsagent's whilst also intimidating him by invading his space. Layton, obeys the rules that Joe had demanded and went into the newsagents and purchased a newspaper of his own choice.

"Now, read the entire first page of the newspaper!" Layton took a brave attempt at reading the newspaper, but still failed miserably as the words appeared as a big blur to him. "I can't read. I just can't do it!" Layton burst into tears, and, before Layton had a chance to explain himself, Joe was already taunting Layton of his disability of not having the capability to read.

"Ha, ha! you can't read! I mean any one can read you're a failure" taunted Joe.

"I'm begging you, please don't tell anyone! Otherwise, everyone will bully me" cried Layton

"Okay, okay! I will not spread the laughter, so long as I can still take fun out of you! Ha ha! I will make your life even more miserable by making you read devices that consist of words and I will punch you every time you fail to read the words out!" Layton sobbed in the far corner of a building that was almost demolished; he remained there until he saw Joe leave the building and then he walked away with tears invading his eyes like an enemy declaring war. Layton had never been so self destructed in all his life; he was now unable to revel in his own existence for he did not feel that he deserved a life at all. "I am not worth a second of any one's time. I protested to Joe how I could read and failed miserably. Now I am a liar as well as a failure." Layton mumbled to himself as he fed himself the repugnant words that lifted themselves into the air, each showing their happy letters.

Chapter 7

The Pleading Beg

Location: Newham House, in Mike's bedroom.
Time: 12/6/2011 Saturday 16:00 pm.

Lou-Lou shouted "Get off the phone! It is urgent!" Mike said "No", and Lou-Lou was so angry!

Lou-Lou, suspicious, strolled into Mike's room innocently, wondering what all of the shouting was about across the phone. It came to Lou-Lou's attention that Mike was talking ignorantly across the phone, making himself oblivious to any action of

Lou-Lou's.

"Why do you have to frustrate me?"

Lou-Lou bellowed in terror as her anger level decreased due to the fact that she was getting really paranoid about what was being established.

"Get off the phone this instant." But, mike says to Lou-Lou "Hold on a minute!" before he can say another word to his friend,

Lou-Lou shouted "Get off of the phone NOW! I have something urgent to tell you and it cannot be delayed any longer!" Lou-Lou cried at the top of her voice in order to be recognised, but she was still ignored by an arrogant Mike.

After consistent begging to get off of the phone, Mike finally followed the order by putting the phone down gently; he knew full well that he was about to receive bad news.

Mike questioned Lou-Lou, "What was

that for?" Lou-Lou answered, "Why did you not tell me that you were doing drugs?"

After that, there was a silent period for about ten seconds when Mike finally piped up. "How did you find out?"

"I lost my charger and I searched the whole house top to bottom looking for it. Then I had a thought, it could be in your room so I searched your whole room until I looked under the bed.

That's when I came across a box which I picked up and it rattled as I shook it, that is when I found my charger, so I opened the box, which I picked up and rattled as I shook it.

I opened the box and, to my surprise, I found the drugs as well as my phone charger underneath. Mike had a guilty expression and begged Lou-Lou.

"Swear you will NEVER tell anyone in your life. Promise?" "I promise not to tell anyone, since you are my brother and I will do anything to protect you". Lou-Lou's reply was slightly inspirational.

When the awkward atmosphere had came to a halt, the conversations grew and grew as the pair began to argue. Instead of dismissing the case, Lou-Lou was persistent as to making Mike confess to his addiction to drugs, followed by helping his addiction to drugs.

"I know everything, so there is no need to tremble with lies! I know that you have been dealing with drugs, which is why I want you to confess face-to-face that you have committed acts against the law. Our entire career could go downhill if you are found out! Do you not even care?"

Instead of even attempting words, Mike stood on two solid feet that could barely keep him to the ground at that present moment.

"I could not help it, I was in distress! What else could I have done?"

One would have thought that such argument would have came to a close within two hours of fighting. How very wrong they would have been. It was made evidential that mike did not at all have any valid reasons or excuses to have been dealing with drugs, which infuriated Lou-Lou all the more. After having been through a rebellious experience already, Lou-Lou did not want to be involved in any more incompetence that would contain acts against the law.

Chapter 8

Approached

Location: The market stall on the Isle of Dogs.
Time: 13/6/2011 Sunday 3pm

The stall was about two square metres, with the merchandise stacked on boxes of other merchandise. Darren was outside of the stall, and walking down the street. Darren is on his own with none of his other friends with him.

Darren is walking down the old street and he saw a strange figure. The weather was cloudy with some sunshine, it was also cold, dark and damp.

It was about 6pm on a Friday evening. Darren was looking for anyone with business ideas because his stall was falling apart slowly, but gradually. The street was covered in filth and dust, it looked as though it had seen better days. There were food wrappers, smashed eggs all over the place and the pavement was cracked and smashed into little pieces (which was all over the place)this is because it is very old. It was starting to look like the stall was a dustbin. Now it looked like nobody would want to buy from here.

There was a strange figure wearing a black hood which looked eerie. He wore grey jogging bottoms and he wore big, black and white Adidas shoes, smelly, and he also had a black cap on. He looked very rough and mean;he was very conspicuous. Darren was thinking that he did not look right so he carried on walking down the wrecked street quietly. The figure was tall, approximately 6 foot, and had a black and orange cool skateboard which had a massive skull on it. The man looked seventeen years old, if not a bit older.

The strange figure saw Darren and told him to stop and walk with him. They sat on a bench which had wood starting to disintegrate and the figure whispered his name it was Dave and then Darren was asked a question. It was a very weird question so Darren thought to himself this person doesn't look good at all, he thought he should just walk away and leave it all alone. But then he had a genius idea...

Dave said surprisingly to Darren "Hello there, I saw you walking down the street and I was wondering if you wanted to buy some phones". Darren thought purchasing these phones would be a good idea if he bought them. He could sell them on his number one stall and make even more money than he made at present, from selling these phones to people for a good and higher price so that he could earn a profit. "Well I do need to make more money so it might be a good idea" answered Darren thinking attentively.

"Yes, you can make alot more money so I think it's a good idea. Is it deal or no deal?"

"Well I shouldn't take things from strangers because it isn't a bright idea as you may be an opposing character underneath, omitting to what I see on top." Darren answered wisely, keeping his head held high at all times.

"Your name is Darren Rodgers, right?" "Dave replied deviously." "How do you know that?" hollowed Darren Shockingly. "We're friends, so is it a deal" Dave calmly replied, hoping it was a smart move. "Well"

Said Darren still unsure.

"Listen, I have to go and get the phones. You better say yes, because you don't want to disappoint a GOOD friend right? "Dave declared whilst being intimidating. All of a sudden Dave walked away slowly.

"Hey, wait up!" shouted Darren, still unsure with his offer. Dave had all ready gone. Darren was surprised at how quickly Dave had disappeared. It was kind of like a miracle. Darren knew that he would return though it wasn't long before he did.

Chapter 9

The Struggle

Location: The market stall, Isle of Dogs.
Time: Monday 14/6/2011. 16:00am

The stall was two square metres in size, with the merchandise stacked on top of red, yellow and blue boxes full of other merchandise. The sky was cold, dull grey due to clouds, it looked like it could rain at any minute. There were barely any customers and it didn't look like there would be any for a long time.

The owners of the stool are realising the stool is not going too good as they expected it would.

"There is no more people coming" Realised Layton. "But were the best shop in town!, we can't be failing now." Cried out Lou Lou. "Whats all the fuss about?" Shouted Darren curiously.

"Wheres all the people, wheres our costumers?" Demanded Darren. "I'm sorry but I think no one likes our shop any more" said Joe with a depressive tone of voice. Everybody started to panic. They tried to think of a plan about how they could get back into business.

"We can't do this anymore!" Whispered Lou-Lou. "Yeah were only kids! I think its a brain buster for us" complained Joe. Everyone was depressed, There were currently below average. Darren was starting to try and help out. but he couldn't think of anything.

Thousands of questions came bursting

into his head. Will a customer come? Will we make even more cash? Do we have to close down the stall? Darren's brain was whirling. What to do, he thought. What to do.

"Any luck yet? Any people?" Asked Darren desperate for the answer to be yes. "No, no luck yet" whined Layton. A tear appeared in to the corner of Darren's eye."I think we might have to think about closing the stall down" Cried Lou-Lou.

"look, We might be in luck!", screamed Joe.

A bunch of people were walking through London town.

"Everyone Cross your fingers for luck!", Layton said excitedly.

Here they came speed walking through the town. Darren opened his mouth in a terrifying gasp. The people just walked straight past. They didn't even give a glance at their brilliant stall. It was like we were imaginary, maybe even invisible.

"I guess, well um " said Layton.

An hour later every one was standing there looking bored and useless, standing in the freezing cold.

"I can't do this any more" Whispered Lou Lou. in a very quiet voice.

"Me either it's to freezing" Replied Joe.

"well I guess I can't either" Said Layton sounding depressing.

"WE CAN'T JUST GIVE UP!" screamed Darren in anger. Every one just stared at Darren.

"So what can we do now then"

"the best thing to do is not to worry"

"so what Shall we do"

they knew he was starting to lose it, So they tried to calm him down. Then discussed what they should do.

"I think we should stop" Said Joe.

"This is to stressing for me I agree with Joe" Replied Lou-Lou.

"Okay the shop is now closed... forever" Said Darren.

He was just about to cry but he held it in. Now they have made allot of money, they are proud of their little success. Everybody is unhappy with their choice but it is for the best, and every one knows that.

Chapter 10

An Inspiring Resolution

Location: In the library in Poplar.
Time: Tuesday 15/6/2011 14:40pm.

The library is quite large, about 19 square metres, with aisles full of shelves full of books, all the way from J. K Rowling to Mark Twain and Shakespeare to top gear. In the centre is the counter where the books are checked out, with the surrounding aisles encircling it. The library is half full, with people at computers, while others are checking the books out, while lots of other people are sitting down and reading. The librarians are stacking books and they are checking the books out for people. There are posters with famous celebrities inside the library promoting people to read. The Library itself is Stratford Library, located on the A11. It is a sunny day, but it isn't hot.

Charlie pulled up outside the Library with his cherry red Ferrari. Carrying three brightly coloured books that he was to return to the library. He didn't enjoy them very much and was disappointed with the quality of the texts. He just stepped into a massive library which was unusually quiet and empty. Just as he gave back the books he noticed out of the corner of his eye a young teen engrossed in a book.

Layton is in the library mostly all the time. The book that he was reading was for children aged 4-5yr old, Charlie was confused and unsure why Layton was reading a book with those age ratings. This was about the wonder-full alphabet which only had 6 pages with one letter on each page. It was a huge shock to see this. He never really used to talk about the really good books that he ever read any way.

Charlie approached Layton and questions.

"Why are you reading that book?" Layton is surprised and embarrassed by this.

"What this book is about three ugly donkeys." Charlie says

"No its not it is about the wonder full alphabet"

"But I thought it was about three ugly donkeys" Layton was very surprised and shocked by this.

"Can you read young man?" Charlie felt very rude for asking the question, but he had an hunch about the young man... and it was worth a try.

"No well I don't know because when I was little I didn't go to school."

"Well do you want some help with that?"

"yes please thank you"

"Well do you want me to tutor you"

Layton felt gratitude wash though him in a wave.

"yes please that will be great thank you so much".

Layton was very grateful to Charlie. Their relationship grew stronger, as Layton never had a father figure in his life. He looked up to Charlie as his father. Charlie didn't have a relationship with his own son, what he did have, was rough. Mike seemed to be growing on Layton. They were starting to act like a real family now, and were growing on each other. All they needed to do was spend some more time together and that wasn't a problem. But I guess they had a rough start, it might just work out for them. They may be a real family for once, but for all you know something could go wrong, and break their hearts. Again...

Chapter 11

Agreement

Location: The end of the street where the market is, away from the stalls, in a more private' Isle of Dogs.
Time: Wednesday 16/6/2011 11:00am.

Dave returned and he snuck up behind Darren.

"Darren how about the offer on the phones?" whispered Dave. Dave walked slowly around Darren, who was wearing black rubber gloves. It was kind of strange.

"I do not know", choked out Darren.

"It's 5, also a very good phone, come

on you know you want it", said Dave in a scary, but intimidating voice.

Darren looked around to see if any one else was there... but they were all alone. "Well I better get my dog some food. He looks hungry", complained Darren. Darren started to walk away, but Dave raised a hand so he would stop. Darren had sweat dripping down his four head. "So deal?", squeaked Dave.

"I saw your stall; is it going well?" asked Dave, trying to change the subject.

"Well not as good as I expected. That's why I need to sell that phone so I can help make it more popular" Darren established.

"Well" said Darren. "I'm still unsure. I might let you. What kind of phone is it? I would love if it was an HTC" slowly said Darren. Darren's dog was starting to pull the leash. "Stop that!" screamed Darren.

"So is it a deal? You know you want to", said Dave in a very convincing voice.

"You do know that it has lots of free games. It is a touch screen, a lovely big iPhone just for you" whispered Dave. "Well I guess it's a deal", said Darren. Darren still wasn't sure. But he wanted to help out, and a HTC for 5! What a good deal! They usually cost hundreds. Darren didn't know that the phones Dave gave him were stolen. That's why Darren took the phone without hesitation.

Dave handed over the shiny multi coloured HTC Wildfires in a huge brown box. "So that will be 5 then" spoke Dave. Darren gave Dave a new five pounds note. A big grin spread on Dave's face. "Have a nice day", whispered Dave in Darren's ear. "Thank you", said Darren, still shaking with fear. They both shook hands, and walked away in the opposite direction.

Dave was putting a lot of pressure on Darren, so eventually he gave in. He took the phones from Dave and just left, walking away from Dave. He took stolen phones he couldn't believe it. That was the first time he had taken stolen goods. But the thing is he didn't really steal them, Dave did. But the thing is now Darren has the stolen phones so he would get the blame.

If he were to get caught there would be no way in the world where Dave would get the blame for the stolen phones he had given to him. He knew that it was the worst mistake he had ever made but he really wanted to open his own phone shop. He could still get rid of the phones and forget it ever happened but he couldn't. He took the phones shaking like a leaf.

He could take the risk of opening his own phone shop or he could take the risk of being caught and the police finding out and he might get arrested. Although he might possibly get arrested he could let this opportunity go by or take it and possibly get arrested. He didn't care about getting arrested he took the phones and carried on walking with great confidence.

The idea in the cafe was an incredible idea and opened his phone shop anyway. He opened the shop and he felt really proud of himself. And so were the other boys - except for Joe. Joe still had his dough ts about the shop but got happier and happier and started to feel happy about the shop and the shop started to become successful.

Now all of the boys like the shop including Joe which was quite hard to believe. Darren was worried even though how confident he was he still felt sick everyday they opened because he kept thinking about the phones he had taken from Dave. He thought that it might be a problem with the police because they are really good at finding out what bad things happen in towns.

Knowing that he was giving random people stolen phones made him feel really bad because they might get the blame and they will get arrested and not Darren, OR DAVE.

Darren started to get really angry but could not have the courage to tell the others why. But the thing is if he left it much longer the police were going to find out and Dave might tell them. That day all through the day that was the only thing that was going through Darren's mind and he just couldn't get it out. Which he thought was very irritating. Darren started to get really intense. But then he looked around and saw his very own shop he couldn't believe it. He was thinking to himself "look at how successful this place is". He was amazed a how well it turned out to be.

Even if it was illegal. But he still felt very guilty because he was selling illegal phones. He hands never stopped shivering the whole day round. All he kept thinking about was getting into huge trouble. To be honest Darren even wondered how Dave got the phones and where.

"They might have came from a warehouse but how would he get in." Darren knew that there was something wrong because there is usually lots of people wondering about the warehouse. How did he know it was going to be easy or hard. It made Darren feel a bit weird. Especially at his age. Darren stopped talking as Dave walked through the door.

Chapter 12

Let the Bullying Commence

Location: Warehouse where they keep the phones in Millwall.
Time: 10/6/2011 Thursday 16:00pm.

The warehouse is fifty square feet in area, connected to other warehouses, the only way to get in is by automatic remote controlled garage door. Inside is boxes full of the phones, there are so many types of phones there's blackBerry, i phones, Samsungs and much more. The boxes are stacked on top of each other, there is only one way into the warehouse, and that is through the full least twenty boxes full of them. The walls are snot green, and the ceiling is four metres high, there are windows three metres high, and they go all the way up to the roof. The lights are dangling of the ceiling, being supported by metal cylinders, there are lights going back in two columns, all the way to the back of the warehouse, starting from the front. There is one light switch to power them all, the switch's casing has cob-webs on, but no spiders. Any open space on the ceiling is covered by cob-webs. Not all the warehouse is lighted by the lights, there is some dark spots, as well as some damp patches where the roof is leaking.

A great hall like structure with high ceilings, and abandoned carts stacked in the corner. Layton walks into the warehouse, sensing the uneasy air about it. He scans the surroundings and spots a black plastic bin-bag. "Something is definitely not right, I can feel it in my bones." Layton whispered the suspicions to himself, nervous twitches agitating Layton.

"Something doesn't seem right. How can all of these phones just appear here and be sold for such a cheap price that everybody would pay? "

The questions circulated Layton's head, drowning in his suspicions. With slight reluctance as to picking up the mobile phones to sell at the stall. Layton patrolled the warehouse, contemplating the stacks of various phones that caught his eye. Casually he reached out for the bin-bag; with prudence he held it in his arms tightly like a baby to it's mother. Which made him feel inner guilt to a certain extent of feeling like a convict himself. After having gathered together approximately hundreds of phones, Layton exited the warehouse fully satisfied. He had a gut instinct that he was committing an act against the law, but it did not at all come into consideration that he was conducting a major outbreak. Layton knew that he would have to repeat the process once again as he could not fit all of the items in such diminutive vehicle all in one go. Layton made sure that he went through with the secretive process in a discreet manner in order to avoid getting held up with police.

After hours of worrying about whether he should return to the warehouse or not, Layton followed his footsteps back to the warehouse in order to collect the remainder of the load of phones which he was unable to collect the first time around.

Examining the warehouse which Layton could conclude as approximately fifty square feet wide, it came to Layton's attention that the person he was purchasing the phones off of was not at all present at the scene.

This startled Layton all the more as he could tell that he was being stitched up in some sort of intellectual process. However, he continued with his actions as he was determined to impress his peers by getting them a whole new stack of phones which could earn them all a living.

With all hands full, Layton went backwards and forwards to the vehicle in which he found himself loading phones in to. Layton continued going backwards and forwards to the condemned vehicle in order to make sure that he was getting what he had paid for. After having spent all of his money on the phones, he was hopeful as to making sure that a vast majority of the stock sold for a reasonable price in order to make up for the costs. Layton managed to unload all of the phones in an orderly manner which assured Layton of success due to the fact that he knew that he had

been very perceptive about the entire process as a whole.
'

"You must be insane!, You do know that you are going to get us all locked up if we are ever found out!" Instead of opposing the opinion, Layton continued with his actions, positive that all would work out in the end. After Layton had finished unloading all of the items out of the colossal warehouse, he grinned with anticipation as to coming back regularly for ongoing stock in order to sell phones at a market stall. Joe did not at all propose to the idea and evolution due to the fact that he was a good guy when it came to playing by the rules.

"Ha! You bunch of twits!, You think that you could all run a stall by yourselves by going against the law? you could not even kill a fly, let alone disobey the law!"

Joe began to taunt his peers with remarks belittling them all, despite the fact that Joe was also part of the plan that he referred to as "pathetic".

After minutes of inspiration, Joe finally collected himself to his feet and made sure that he was contributing to the plan as much as he did not agree with it. Joe compromised by working coordinately with his team in order to achieve excellence by the end of life.

"Layton, go through the entire check list on the clipboard in order to make sure that everything has been collected together. Remember, we have to make sure that we precede in this business in a discrete manner as we do not want this to be a failure in the end by getting caught by the police."

Layton reluctantly went through the clipboard as Joe had demanded, ensuring that nothing had been left out.

Chapter 13

Nice Day at the Market

Location: The market stall in the Isle of Dogs.
Time: Saturday 19/6/2011 13:00pm.

It is a bright Sunny day on West Ferry road at the Isle of dogs. There are customers surrounding the whole of the stall, all pushing and barging past each other to get what they can, while they can.

"Good afternoon," shouted Lou-Lou.

"Have a nice day and thank you for coming" Joe shouted enthusiastically to the costumer.

"We are doing excellent!" exclaimed Layton.

"WOW! You've made millions" Said Darren in a surprised voice.

"We're going to be swimming in money soon" Joked Joe in a jolly voice. "Hey look it's Dave".

"I think he's got the stuff for you" Said Lou-Lou.

"I knew this place would go down well." said Darren in a proud tone of voice.

Darren was really glad to think of this idea. He was even surprised the idea went well even though he was expecting this. Suddenly an entire crowd of customers stormed towards their stall.

The stall was flooding with people and they didn't know what to do. They had to think quickly otherwise there will be nothing left of it. There was lots of people being served at the same time and that made it really hard for them to concentrate.

They managed to keep up with some of the customers but in the end it was to hard so they had tell people to leave. There wasn't even any room to move so there was no other choice but to make them move. It had taken them a very long time to get out of the shop because they just refused to leave.

Then now it had taken them even longer to get out because they were running around the shop. It was like a wild goose chase to get them out. Then they started to threaten the man by pretending to ring the police. But that did not work so they just ran after him and when they eventually got him out of the shop they were all laying on the floor breathing really heavily. They didn't want to open the shop just until a few hours. had past.

A few hours past and they opened the shop back up just to see that very same man who they were tried to get out for about three hours. They knew he was going to get mad again so they try to close the gate as fast as they could. But sadly he quickly slid on his stomach back under the gate and he started to charge around the shop again.

Before they even attempted to chase him out of the shop again they sat down and just breathed because they knew they were going to need it with this gentlemen. The guy had kind of a weird looking face as if he had just been to the pub. His face was bright red his hair was scruffy and his back was bent over like he was just gonna charge at us. Until he did. He actually started to run after them. In there own shop. So they just went with it and they just ran screaming as loud as they could and running as fast as they could. They had no clue what to do. There only hope was to open the gate and hope that someone would come in and help but no. Not a single soul came in to help them with that awful and weird looking man. It was like nobody even cared about them and it was just a bit of fun. Except they were running for there lives and someone was hiding under the desk.

Finally the weird man stopped running after us. But the thing was, he just stood there staring. And they started to get even more scared because they didn't know what he was thinking. Then he just ran out the door.

"PHEW!, lucky we escaped." they all said with a sigh of relief. They quickly shut the shop gate down and didn't open it till the next day just to make sure they were safe.

"Hello Dave, what a nice moment to see you" Said Darren.

"Here I have got a box of things you can sell at the stool, I still get some money right?" Said Dave, continuously.

Darren didn't know if he was joking or not, because it is quite rude to just say that to some one.

"You can get a few notes" Said Darren still wondering if he was joking. But Dave didn't laugh he just stood there with a blank expression on his face.

"Well back to work" Screeched Dave. Would an ordinary person ask for money?

"Sir yes sir" thought Darren. Darren carried the big box which Dave gave to him.

"Quick people, we need to make more money than that!" Mentioned Darren, in a slightly encouraging voice. "why!"

"because."

"yes u definitely"

"were on fire!" boomed Joe.

"The pot of money is going to explode, imagine what we can buy a limo a mansion a holiday to Spain another limo" Lou Lou said in a very joyful voice.

"We still have lots more to sell" fused Joe.

"Help I'm drowning in the costumers - there are so many of them!" laughed Lou Lou.

"I think we're going to need another pot for the money" Smiled Darren.

Everyone was coming up to them raising their money in the air.

"I'll quickly go to the other shop just across the street to get some more phones before we run out!" Screamed Joe at the top of his lungs.

They were selling fast. Every object they had was disappearing. There was only twenty seven more things left. It was starting to get more peaceful, but there was still a few more costumers.

Moments later, Joe came back with a huge pot.

"Put the money in here" insisted Joe.

"We're rich" Screamed Layton.

"I can't believe it. We've done it, we are the most popular shop in town!" Shouted Darren. The four teenagers approved of their business and were all jubilant towards the success of the business that had proved to be a good idea. They were really happy and rich, but all of the phones were stolen.

However, none of them were aware that the phones had not been seized legally; they were indeed stolen. Despite the fact that they possessed no awareness of the phones having been stolen, Joe had a gut instinct all along that there was something not quite right about the products that they had purchased for a reasonably cheap price, for what the phones were worth.

Chapter 14

Silent Treatment

Location: Newham house (Mikes house).
Time: Sunday 20/6/2011 15:00pm.

The stairs lead to the kitchen, where charlie is standing with a cup of coffee. The stairs are laminated oak flooring. There is twenty stairs. The stairs were so clean, they were spotless, like they where brand new. On the wall next to the stairs are paintings, and family portraits of the family. Along with the children's school photos. The hallway leading into the kitchen is a light green wall with ten spotlights on the ceiling, with calendars and a phone on the wall. In some of the photos their mother is holding baby mike, and baby Lou-Lou. As they where three years old, when she died. There is also photos of their mother with charlie, from when they where young, if not weeks before she died.

As Mike came down the stairs in a casual way, he was listening to his music with his earphones in. Just as Mike got to the last step his dad said "Son can you come into the kitchen for a chat please?" "what for" shouted mike in a deep dark voice. "just come please son" screeched charlie. Charlie wasn't looking to satisfied.

But for some reason mike wouldn't talk to charlie "son is there something wrong?" "NO!!!" "well you haven't been talking much and you have been in your bedroom most of the time" "SO what!" screeched Mike "Just tell me Son" "NO!!" This made charlie get extremely furious. He took mikes red and green earphones off him and threw them in the bin with all of the strength he could. So Mike gave charlie the dirtiest look in the world. "how dare you" So Charlie gave mike an even dirtier so you will suffer the consequences."

mike slammed the door with rage running through his veins. "Whats the matter? Why wont he talk to me it can't be that bad can it?" charlie said There was a moment of silence, across the room. Mike just ignored him. Mike paused at the stairs because he thought to himself "now I have to save up for new earphones!!" moaned mike He slammed his bedroom door as loud as a bomb in a house.

Mike felt depressed. It was like he was trapped in a little hole and couldn't get out of it. He started to get tears in his eyes he really missed hes mum. He wanted hes mum's comfort.

Mike thought he was going to have a nervous break down. Tears rapidly rolled down hes face. Mike strolled across to his circled shaped bed covers which had a yellow, green, orange and blue theme to it. Also he layed onto his bed and had a very long cry. Mikes face was pitch white. He looked ill, very ill.

Chapter 15

The Inadequate is Informed

Location:Westferry Road.
Time: Monday 21/6/2011 12:00pm.

It was a fine and harmless day in the streets of London, where all of the corruption and catastrophes usually occurs. One unusual policeman was witnessed patrolling the streets in a suspicious manner, which belittled the four teenagers as they were extremely self conscious about getting caught in the process of stealing.

When it came to realization that four teenagers were on the back of a old red lorry, the policeman darted over to his fellow policewoman, who he knew was a lot more efficient than himself, making him certain that she would tie up any loose ends with the suspicious crime, if there were of course a crime being committed.

Without hesitation, the policewoman questioned the action of the teenagers who were stated and referred to as near future convicts. She was reluctant as to letting the scenario slip; she was full of resolute as to solving the scene once and for all, after having been given an opportunity to question the scene.

"What is there in the back of the van that they could possibly desire, how old are these teenagers?" The policewoman was determined to resolve the situation once and for all, whether it meant life or death. Gazing around and contemplating the scenery of London, the police officer was observing possible clues that could be questionable. When it came to her attention that the foursome were unloading objects from the van, she made herself certain that illegal acts were being conducted. Frightened about the reputation of the city, as well as the incompetence of her individual character, the policewoman acted immediately.

"Excuse me, lads, I would like to know where you got all of these phones from. I do believe that you could not have paid for all of those whilst selling them for a low price and still making a profit."

"We are teenagers, mam! When you look down the street and you see a teenager, what do they always have in their hand? A phone. Together, we have been through many phones and we are now selling, I don't see any harm in that so, if you would be so kind, we have work to do."

Darren deviously talked his way out of

the mishap, but his three companions just looked at him clueless with extreme confusion as to what to do.

"You're telling me that you four teenagers have had thousands of brand new phones between you over your short lifespan? Why, you must be the richest people on Earth! Sorry, but I have to investigate the scenario further in order to reassure myself."

Neither Darren, Lou-Lou or any of the four companions had anything to say to the policewoman's remark, which explained all. The verdict was guilty as soon as she approached the scene, from the policewoman's perspective. The policewoman returned to the spot in which she was patrolling in order to make notes of the scene she had been witnessing. Are the teenagers going to get away with it, or is it a serious crime? who knows!

Chapter 16

The Bullying Continues

Location: Outside Layton's home, which is a flat on whitton walk in poplar.
Time: Monday 21/6/2011 17:00pm.

Joe is Walking and he sees Penny walking to school and sees this as an opportunity to nose-about. Penny is aware of Joe's judging eyes following her and quickens her pace. Realising Penny's intentions, Joe runs after her grabbing her arm so as to stop her from going further. Penny lets out a screech and tries to shake him off, but he has a firm grip on her. Penny starts to panic struggling to break into a run. "Calm down gal! I only wanted to ask you some questions!". She does not listen. She stops screaming and struggling for a few seconds

Joe tried to get Penny's attention "oi you must be Layton's sister err what is it oh yes Penny" Joe said. "Go away!" Penny explained. With yesterday happening, fresh in his mind, Joe decided to pay Layton a visit, but he got more than what he bargained for. As he approached the block of flats on Whitton walk Joe was annoyed at the fact that he was told to go away and started to prod and poke Penny then she started crying.

Layton then walked out the flat and saw Penny crying. When he saw Joe he shouted at him to" "go and jump off a bridge" Joe then slowly walked away smiling in a sorrowful mood. As he's head hurt, and he did feel quite guilty.

Layton said to Penny he was only messing about and that he was lying just to annoy her. Penny was so upset, so she ran inside to get a box of tissues. Layton was on his way to charlies house (who is his tutor) and penny was on her way to school.

Chapter 17

Time for Answers

Location: Market Stall in the Isle of Dog
Time: Tuesday 22/6/2011 14:00pm.

Joanne was standing on the side of an advanced road full of people wondering what all the comotion was about, the policewoman examined the actions of the teenagers who all looked extremely suspicious. Due to the fact that the teenagers looked entirely suspicious as well as they were selling brand new phones for a price that as not at all expected, the policewoman began to scan up and down at the market stall that the four troubled teenagers were in possession of the phones.

A beaming smile and a beam of joy, four troubled teenagers leaped down the road of disasters waiting to happen. Glancing at the benevolence of each citizen, Lou-Lou decided upon committing a crime that she had no idea would result in a total disaster. The foursome gazed at the back of the lorry which was being unloaded by a well built man who was finding the job strenuous. Lou-Lou whispered a brief plan that the four of the adolescents would, co-ordinately, precede.

With ambition present of a higher rate than ever, Lou-Lou approached the back of the van where Lou-Lou found herself standing amongst a whole new world of brand new phones. Dazzled and blinded with greed, she leaped onto the van and attempted committing a crime, when it came to a policeman's awareness that Lou-Lou was up to no good. Within seconds, the policeman had informed another member of the police force of the crime about to be committed, which could be fatal. Without hesitation, the policewoman darted over to the near future convicts, ensuring that they were denied of any escape. The policewoman ran down the street at the speed of light, without hesitation as to giving up. For this reason alone, she could have easily been referred to as a persistent person. The determined policewoman prevented all teenagers, excluding Lou-Lou, from continuing to run by blocking their pathway after having ran at the speed of light from one end of the street to the other.

The ambiguous policewoman questioned the actions of the troubled teenagers that were attempting to commit a serious crime.

Lou-Lou, omitting the actions of her peers, she continued to run away as if it was a life or death scenario. Down the alley of forbid and darkness, Lou-Lou exceedingly ran to the best of her ability, when she overstepped the line between fiction and reality. Her foot tripped over a misplaced traffic cone that was placed in the very centre of the road where danger was just a matter of when, not if. Coming to realization, the policewoman took into account that Lou-Lou had attempted crime, escape and had committed the act without failure.

Chapter 18

Confrontation

Location: Millwall Bridge in London, Millwall Time: Tuesday 22/6/2011 17:00pm

Darren sees Dave and Darren has a bag containing different phones and he says to Dave. "I don't want your stolen phones"

He then throws the phones on the floor and most of them break and shatter into pieces.

"WHY YOU TWERP, WHY I HAVE A GOOD MIND TO-" Dave said. Dave was absolutely fuming.

Dave starts shouting at Darren and he

says,

"Take the phones now or I will make your body crack in many places, or I will beat you until your black and blue!" Claimed Dave.

Dave and Darren burst into a fight on the bridge! Blood and teeth fly everywhere! They stop for a few seconds, and then carry on. Dave then falls off the bridge, luckily for him Darren grabs both his legs but Dave's shoes falls off he then falls in the water beneath. He is drowning in the water splashing as he cant swim. Darren doesn't help him out of the water, Dave drowns to death and Darren puts his body on the street and runs off. he heard the ambulance come speeding down the road with it's signals going off it was the ambulance. The ambulance people quickly got out of the car. They do a quick check up on Dave. There was a sad impression on their face. Silence spread the word. The ambulance people managed to say. Dave is dead. On the dark and gloomy streets of London at 5:00pm the bridge was covered by old tiles in all different locations and shapes. It was very dark and there were clouds everywhere in the sky that looked very evil and menacing looking because the sunset was between two holes in a cloud which made it looking like a evil face in the sky looking at Darren at what had happened. Darren felt bad just leaving Dave there especially knowing that he died. He felt incredibly guilty and didn't know what to do with himself. Whilst Darren ran off and let Dave just sit there lying dead on the side of the road. The ambulance was speeding down the road trying to get to Dave as fast as they could. They got him in the back of the ambulance very quickly and they rushed Dave of to hospital while Darren was running away from the situation. Darren kept running and running and running thinking that he might get the blame for this terrible and horrific accident.

Chapter 19

Family Affairs

Location: Layton's flat in poplar.
Time: Wednesday 23/6/2011 18:00pm.

It was a typical day and everybody was preceding day-to-day life, which usually consisted of regular violence and beatings for one particular family. Layton was speeding down an advanced road that shone its brightness in terms of being the most orderly street within the city. Layton was entirely introverted as he would always remain silent whilst in the presence of his mother. With haunting screams coming from the direction of his house, Layton darted down the road to find that his house had been entirely corrupted with catastrophe.

My knees are shaking with fear at the sight of my own reflection exulting in its existence due to my inner horror that is evidential; I am even more terrified than one could ever be whilst in the presence of a poltergeist. I cannot deny myself of my true emotions and feelings of wanting to be accompanied by a friend during this difficult period. The reality being that I cannot bare life without a companion supporting me twenty-four:seven.

"What had gone on whilst I was absent?" The question remained consistent as he glanced around at the utter chaos. He gazed at the jet black furniture that was witnessed with a gaping hole in it. Precisely where his eyes lied, Layton found himself staring into the eyes of his mother who disapproved of Layton's presence as a result of being entirely drunk that she could not even recall her own name. Layton's face was bowed with disappointment, an emotion all too familiar to him.

"Why are you here?" The angry mother defused her daughter of self esteem by the way in which she demanded that Penny were to leave he room immediately, or else she would suffer the consequences. However, she was already suffering the consequences as Penny was hit to the floor by her drunken mother. Yelling in fear, Layton cried for help as he witnessed such incompetence of his mother, all due to drink.

"Mother, it is my home, remember! All the time you do this to me, all the time! Everyone else is entitled to a mother, whereas I am only entitled to someone who consistently drinks herself sober! "

Layton sobbed as he was raising his voice, although his inspirational speech was of no use as his mother would not even remember it.

"Why can't she just understand?"

Avoiding society, Layton hid in one corner of the room whilst thinking about having a decent mother like all of his friends were entitled to. With all infuriation exulting in his existence, Layton hit his head on the wall with force as he was unable to believe in himself due to the immense difficulty life was conducting; having a constant drunken mother did not at all help the case.

Chapter 20

The Lost Loved One

Location: Newham House, Mike's room.
Time: Thursday 24/6/2011 19:00pm

Mike was sitting down thinking about his childhood, he could only think about the bad things. He looked back to how bad his childhood was. He felt so depressed.

He thought to himself "why can't I just die now?" He felt the need to take some drugs. However, earlier that day he had arranged to meet some friends. He then decided to take a different path. Then he realized the path he was walking on, was the path his mum, dad, sister, and him used to take on the way home from school. It brought back so many memories then he realized his childhood wasn't as bad as he thought, it was apart from the fact his mum and dad always argued mostly about money.

I was three years old and my mum, and my dad, Charlie and my sister Lou-Lou all went to the beach. It was as hot as an oven and there were loads of children around. My mum and I went to get an ice-cream whilst my sister found us a nice spot.

My mum and I came back to see everything was laid out nicely on our beach mat. Then my mum got her kayak and decided to go for a ride in her speed boat. She jumped in and told us that she will be back in five minutes. I saw her ride away in her speed boat.

The engine was roaring as she went. I couldn't see her. She was gone out in sea. I waited for five minutes, but she never came. I waited there for two hours, she did not come back. I stayed with my sister sitting on the beach. I waited there, and a day later I saw my Auntie. Lou-Lou and I were crying. She proclaimed "I'm so sorry... Your mum shes... gone."

Mike woke up realising he was not breathing. He let out a long breath. Mike started to cry. He was so sad the whole of his body was aching. Mike needed help. Serious help, But there was no one around and besides, why would anyone help him. He already had an argument with his dad, and his sister wouldn't help him any way.

All of a sudden, all Mike saw was pitch black. It was like he was staring at a black picture. It was a black as anything you could imagine. Mike thought he was closing his eyes, but a few seconds later he realised he wasn't.

Mike felt like he was empty inside him. He felt like he was fading away. It stayed black and didn't get a touch brighter. He started to become scared because he was the only one there. It was black for miles, it was like it was never going to end.

He called out to see if anyone could hear him but they couldn't. He was certainly the only one there. But he was too scared to give up. He was calling for hours upon hours. And running for miles, and miles.

But still no one to be seen, not a whisper, not a scream, it was all just him. He didn't believe he was the one there he was too scared to think otherwise. He stared into the distance, but it was no use. He wasn't even sure how far he could see in this light. He wasn't even sure if he could see at all.

Then Lou-Lou comes in. Her face was shocked "Hi brother how are...?"

Air was trapped in Lou Lou's mouth. Lou Lou just burst into tears. "HELP! SOME ONE HELP!" screeched Lou-Lou. Mike was dead. Lou-Lou was screaming as she stood there looking at Mike on the floor dead. Mike had a drug overdose.

Mike was on the floor with a really pale face. He looked as white as a ghost. His hair was really scruffy like a long haired guinea pig. Some of it was spread around the floor. There was also a pair of scissors next to him so he might of cut off his own hair. Mike started to stink up the room, and it was so bad it made Lou-Lou cry even more. Lou-Lou couldn't believe that her own brother, was dead lying on the floor.

Lou-Lou ran to her phone. She picked her phone up as fast as she could. She dialled her dads number.

"Answer please, answer" weeped Lou-Lou. "Hello" exclaimed Charlie.

"Dad come down now no questions just come" Lou Lou hung up she froze in terror and tried to think of what to do. She quickly ran down the stairs waiting for her dad to knock at the door. It took a while but eventually he showed up. "WHAT? WHAT'S HAPPENED LOU-LOU?" he shouted. "I, It's Mike, I think he's... dead!" She screamed with fear.

Dad, in a hurry sprinted up the stairs calling Mike's name.

"MIKE MIKE ARE YOU OK?" He bellowed. Then dad ran into the room staring at Mike dead on the floor. He couldn't believe it. Sooner than you would of imagined he burst into tears as well. As they watch there own flesh and blood on the floor by a drug overdose. They very speedily picked up the phone and called the ambulance to come as soon as possible. And when the ambulance came and took Mike took the hospital at great speed and got him his own room.

There was a loud thump at the door. Lou-Lou rushed to the door. "Quick its Mike!" Boomed Lou Lou. Charlie and Lou-Lou saw Mike laying there on the floor.

"He can't be, not now he's, he's only a kid!" Wailed Charlie. ,

Charlie bursts into tears and Lou Lou and charlie have a talk Charlie and Lou Lou both burst into tears. They sat there hugging each other, hoping that this dreadful moment would just go and they could be a happy family again.

"I guess it's over." cried Lou-Lou.

"Yes it is" Sniffled Charlie.

"We will remember him forever" They both declared.

They both lit a candle and prayed for he's spirit. They will get he's funeral in a couple of weeks, and will soon find out how bad he's drug taking was. Lou-Lou knew that he was going to overdose and it happened, happened today.

Chapter 21

Getaway

Location: The Market stall.
Time: Sunday 27/6/2011 16:25pm.

When it came to realization that the phones could not have possibly been purchased legally without loosing money, the policewoman made a cunning plan; she 3 approach the teenagers in order to make sure that her conclusion was correct in terms of not being judgemental.

As well as stereotypical towards the younger generation of teenagers. They all appeared to be full of enlightenment at the sight of buckets full of money that could allow them each to buy themselves a brand new car.

The policewoman had a vague frown upon her face as she disapproved of the act that should never have been committed. She knew full well that they were not earning money through legal definitions, which forced her to approach them in a subtle manner.

With a by passer warning the policewoman that the teenagers were up to no good, the policewoman did not hesitate as to approaching the teenagers in order to question their actions.

"How did you manage to get hold of all these phones in such perfect condition, without loosing money?" Asked the policeman she patrolled the stall with deep contemplation towards the expression and guilt upon each and every member's faces.

She had a gut instinct that they were

making acts against the law due to the fact that nobody would sell phones for a really cheap price when they were worth a lot more than they were actually being sold for, meaning an immense loss of money would have been made.

The policewoman is standing in the street and and a police constable informs her that four teenagers are committing a crime consisting of stolen phones in the back of some lorries so the policewoman investigates the crime and sees the four teenagers.

The four teenagers are running from the policewoman as fast as they can, like a cheetah runs to catch her pray for her cubs.

The policewoman pulls out a stun gun attached to her belt and she attempts to shoot one of them and just hits the person, but it falls off the person.

They get a nasty shock they then start

limping because of the sharp end of the projectile which sends the shock, which can be as bad as the stun itself.

Chapter 22

The Saviour

Location: Westferry Road, Isle of Dogs.
Time: Sunday 27/6/2011 16:35pm.

The street lights are few in numbers, as well as any light at all. The streets have patches of litter on, and the street is abandoned. Dogs are barking, and foxes are screeching.

There are multiple side roads leading out from the main Road (West ferry road) to separate other housing estates. As they run down West ferry road, they take a right down Harbinger road, then take the first left down Marsh street, then turn left again to get back to West ferry road, in a desperate attempt to lose the police. They carry on running down the road when they duck into the west ferry metro, which is the local newsagent.

Layton looked behind him and saw the policewoman. "Quick the policewoman is catching up!" Layton and Joe started to gain speed. They really didn't want to get captured

My senses heighten. Every snapping twig sends jolts through my spine. My head instinctively turns in the direction of sound. My head throbbing, I can no longer tell up from down. Neck strained, their bones creaking like rusty hinges. If but to be a bird and soar free, but sooner than later the screeching bullet fired will take me down. I run but I cannot hide. No cover, no shelter just a straight stretch of cold concrete. And suddenly the distance to safety seems never-ending. How much further will my legs take me? The hot blood pushes through the veins in my legs, the friction leaving it sore and bruised. Numb.

A scream shatters my train of thought and for a second I stop to look. My legs turn to jelly and threatens to collapse. Bright lights are flooding through in the distance. The dark concrete is now a carpet laid with glittering crystals. And I hear the rumbles and roars of engines as they speed towards us. My legs start to falter, Joe takes the lead and hurries forward. That's when it happened... The next series of events played itself in slow-motion and the outcome of it all seemed clear to me. As if acting with instinct, my brain disregarded the fact that my legs were about to fall off. A sudden lurch threw my body forwards, My arms searching for his. Dazzled by the car lights as it swallows us whole; only to wake face down on the pavement. My mind a blur as I try to process what has happened, a sudden sickness overwhelms me as I imagine the worst. Blood, metal and pale faces. Joe leans forward and gently shakes Layton, he calls out to him wide-eyed and teary. "Layton! Please, for goodness sake... say something". He hangs his head in shame and curses under his breath. *It takes a while for my head to come round. The left side of my face is sweaty and swollen, the blood salty in my mouth.* Pulling himself together Layton plucks himself off the ground, dusted-off, he wipes the blood off his face with the back of his sleeve and stretches out a hand to the still kneeling Joe. He looks up with mixed emotions: Awe, fascination, confusion, pride and most of all respect. Taking Layton's hand was the first step to the beginning of a new friendship. They walked in awkward silence, alone on the street, it seems they've dodged the police. Joe has been wracking his mind for 20 minutes now, he has never thought so hard in his life, he has never had to. Layton walked beside him, calm, with a look of emptiness on his face...lost in a world of his own though not quite day-dreaming, more meditating. Joe coughs to break the silence. "Err Layton...thanks man, what you did...back there, err...it was great. You saved my life and I know I've been hard on you, but I don't really have friends. They usually just use and abuse me. Guess I should have known better. So er...thanks". Joe was relieved, his hard thinking had paid off. Layton still stayed silent, leaving Joe to contemplate whether he was expecting a reply. "Er just wondering', why did you save me?". "It's what you would have done for me, isn't it", Layton said, his gaze fixed at the road ahead. Joe flushed, staring at Layton's face while they walked side-by-side. He nodded. "Yeah course".

Chapter 23

...and...

Both Layton and Joe were in bad shape. His shoulder blade was sodden with hot dark blood. Like ink, it spread across the light blue cotton hoody, decorating it with splashes of deep maroon. His head ringing, as if loud bells were bashing in his head. Layton spotted a police van although it took him a long time to read he notified Joe and they both slipped into an off licence. They hid while the police men walked past with their companions.

Drooling like hungry mammals, teeth baring, clenched paws beating against the earth below. Bred like hunters. In a league of their own, a policeman's best friend. He let out a long and deep sigh of relief, "I thought you couldn't read? guess you're not that thick". Smirks crept on the sides of both their faces, lip curled they giggled and for a split second everything was good. Wanting too hold the moment forever, forever is a long time, forever is a myth'

Chapter 24

Disaster Strikes

Location: Trinity Hospital Near Woolwich Road.
Time: Sunday 27/6/2011 9:15pm.

Flashing lights dominate the scene in front of me. All things happening at once, the city has never been so restless. Sleeplessness prevails tonight as all the back-door mischief builds up to this very event. Sea blue and fluorescent yellow checked police cars pile at the end of the road. Screeching tires give off the smell of smoking rubber. And the fumes settle like a fog over the once still Woolwich road.

The chaos has only added to the resounding pounding in the suffocating space we call our head. The men in uniform bound towards the already pinned suspects, falling into their designated places like a regular routine work-out. I stand with Joe silent beside me, not having the audacity to shift from the shadows. For now it is our haven. The perfect place to have a look-see without being earmarked. Guilt is no longer an issue, fear has compelled us rooted to the spot. We won't move.

I don't know what's worse. . . watching your friends getting arrested - or knowing that you had a part to play in it.

Hands cuffed, Darren is shoved into the back of a car, being beaten down by foul words. His face sweaty and pale, a look of bewilderment as he stares out of the tinted glass window. My mind urges me to do the right thing. I want to run! Run towards him with open arms and let him know that I'll be there with him, all the way... But my legs do not move; they don't even hesitate. Heartless as they are, I feel my mind disconnected from my body. Either that or the electrically excitable neurons carrying the commands of my brain to my body, have reached a brick wall. And a brick wall it was. As I watched my friend, my fellow shop-mate, unwillingly driven off to the police station. Guilt forms a knot in my stomach It could have been me in the back of that car'.

"Please officer I didn't know... I swear it, I never knew what they were doing. Where they were getting the phones from." Lou-Lou was terrified and pleaded her innocence whilst being driven to the hospital. "Sorry darlin', you can save it for the court", mumbled the officer in charge. As he dazed out of the little rectangular window in the back of the ambulance, he could see the flashing lights of the police cars tailing them. Lou-Lou was helpless, talking to the policeman wouldn't work, he didn't seem too concerned about the given situation. "What about my dad? Will he know... oh no, he's going to be out of his mind!", she couldn't help but to panic. Everything that could go wrong has gone wrong and there was nothing she could do about it. "Course he'll know. He'll be notified once you're in temporary custody." The officer snickered slightly. *Ah kids, always getting into trouble... did they honestly think they would get away with it? Regret plays on the minds of those who have lost the most. Invading their personal thoughts, and rendering their dreams a nightmare.*

Layton and Joe turn back the way they came. The long walk gave them time to think. So much has happened within two weeks, it was too much to fathom. Lives were lost, crimes committed, friends hurt. They never intended for the situation to spiral out of hand. Nobody was ever in complete control. They hadn't a clue what they were doing; and the price had to be paid, for when there are crimes there are always consequences. *I find myself torn. Torn between my emotions, not knowing what to feel, what should I feel? I have never let myself lose composure. To let my disposition show; no longer am I in control. I am but a puppet. How selfish have I been to myself, to lock away these unknown feelings. And how sad it is that now I will not feel each of them intimately, but rush through them as though it were a file yet never reading them. Still I find comfort in knowing I have someone walking beside me, that if I should faint from the exhaustion of emotion, there will be a hand. I cannot predict what the future holds for me, but I know now how I will go about my future. Who I will be. How I will be. It is times like these when I can back-track and remember what it felt to be a child. Though that was robbed from me long ago. I remember wading in the snow on a fresh crisp winter morning, my mothers warm fingers wrapped around my mitten-covered hands. I remember sitting on the swings in the park; the summer oozy and warm as I blissfully gaze at my first crush as she swung backwards and forth beside me. I remember climbing onto the cot where my round and well-wrapped sister lay in a bundle, snoozing the day away... And then I remember no more... How the wheel can turn so quickly I have never understood. All I know is if you're not prepared then you never will be. I watched as my life turned from amazing to disappointing. She had given up at the first signs of trouble. Growing up after that happened twice as fast, adapting is nature's way after all. If ever I need a reminder of who I want never to be, I need look no further than my porch... she was dead to me long ago. Hatred turns a heart black, forgiveness can heal that. He has yet to forgive her.* Their faces expressed sheer disgust as they hauled the body out of the water. Motionless, with pale clammy yellow coloured skin. The skin now as fragile as tissue paper as it gently peeled off showing the gloopy flesh beneath. Eyes still wide open, as if frozen in time, the expression of horror remained stiff on his face. Big and bulging and pitiful as they sulked, lifeless and still.

"Yes this is definitely the suspects body. That's Dave Blanche." The policewoman replied through the walkie-talkie, her voice heavy with despair.

"What have I done, I never meant for him to fall off. He just...slipped. "Hot tears clouded Darren's vision, after confessing to the police they had brought him along to help with the search. He choked on his saliva, forcing himself to stay composed. "A man never cries", he whispered to himself, as if to alleviate himself. Trying to rid of this sudden stab of pain he felt. But he crumbled, on his hands and knees, fumbling towards the dead body weeping as the realisation of what he had done finally struck him. It struck him hard in the chest. He had taken a life. And what right had he to do so...

There were many ways in which these events could have played out. Bad choices, blindness by greed and the thirst for more drove it in the direction of destruction. As it shows the bitter calamities leading to the end.

"All good things must come to an end."
-Alexandre Dumas, The Three Musketeers

Character Profiles

Darren
Darren is 17 years old and never leaves the house without his dog Poochie, who is a great Dane. He's part of a tight-nitt group of friends with Layton, Joe, and Lou-Lou.

Layton
Layton is 17 years old and always out and about doing active things - you'll never catch him with his nose in a book when he could be out in the fresh air...

Charlie
Charlie is 54 years old. He is the father of Lou-Lou and Mike, he runs a successful

business and we have a dog called Spike who is an Alsatian. He fears he is losing touch with his kids but will help out anyone.

Mike
Mike is Lou-lou's big brother, he is 17-years old and and enjoys playing football, he thinks his dad should stop bothering him and let him live his own life.

Lou-Lou
Lou-Lou is Charlie's daughter and Mike's little sister. She wears blue ripped jeans, red and white checked shirts with vests underneath her shirts Her favourite hobby is judo, which she has a yellow belt in.

Joe
Joe is 19 years old, and strong - he loves fishing in France. He likes Hollister clothes

and can be mean to his friends - they appear to put up with him though...

Dave
Dave is 16 years old who seems very attached to his black hoody, very much a shady character - he always appears to be up to something. He has the mind of a villain and doesn't take no for an answer.

Joanne
Joanne is a 26 years old policewoman, she is introverted when it comes to meeting new people, but aggressive when dealing with domestic violence. Joanne is an easy-going person with a lot of charisma! She enjoys helping the community and meeting new people. Joanne is Layton's Nephew.

The Authors

Haig Spalding
My name is Haig Spalding - I am twelve years old and like to read books. I love science but my favourite subject is English. I like horror and thriller/crime books, and my favourite books are the Beast Quest series because they are really enjoyable - if you like action they are great books for you. My favourite hobby is fishing.

Courtney Richards
I am eleven years old and I have a pet cat. My favourite colour is blue and my favourite subject is P. E. I love chocolate, and my favourite drink is Dr Pepper, which makes me very hyper. I have

brown, shoulder length hair with a fringe and I have hazel eyes. I like Science only when it's Chemistry.

Ryan Jones

My name is Ryan Jones; I am fourteen years old. I enjoy watching Formula 1, and I love playing video games. I don't watch any football, except international football, and only when England is playing. When I am older I would love some kind of tattoo on my back - I have two ideas already. I don't really know what I want to do when I am older, but my dream jobs would be to be a formula 1 driver or to be in the British S. A. S.

Sam Homewood

I am eleven years old and I like to play football with my friends. I joined this project because I really like English and I thought it would be an amazing opportunity to write my own book with some my friends. *And* I got to get out of lessons for a week. My dream job is a cartoon artist or policeman.

Laura Ash

I am eleven years old and I love animals, especially dolphins, I think bottle nose dolphins are the cutest. My hair colour is dark brown, I have brown eyes and I'm very tall. I love tormenting my big brother Ant (he's 22 years old).

Ryan King

My name is Ryan King. I am thirteen years old. I was born on 20th August 1998 at Gravesend Hospital. I enjoy playing my Nintendo Wii and Xbox 360. I wanted to do this project because I thought it would be a great opportunity for me and it's great to be so proud about my work.

Katie Sharp

My name is Katie Sharp, I am in year seven and am eleven years old. I did this project because it would be great to be the first people of our age to have done this so quickly!

Tommie Taylor

My name is Tommie Taylor, I am thirteen years old. I like to play first-person shooter games on my Xbox. My favourite type of films are horror, action and comedy films - particularly ones with zombies!

Bethany Bennett

My name is Bethany Bennett, I am thirteen years old and enjoy doing Judo. This project has made me believe in myself much more and I am more confident as a result of this week.

Katy Smith
My name is Katy Smith and I am a fourteen year old student who admires English, especially when it comes to writing my own novels and poems. I have always dreamed of publishing my own novel and this week was the very week in which my dream became reality. My hobbies are reading and writing, which are the the essentials in my life. As much as I also love acting, English has always been my priority as it is my favourite subject.

Hidayah Mustafa
My name is Hidayah Hameem Mustafa, I am fourteen years old and my favourite subjects are English, Art and the sciences. My favourite colours are red and purple, and I like playing netball, writing poetry

and reading.